Vampire Child

Paul Blum

RISING STARS

NASEN House, 4/5 Amber Business Village, Amber Close,
Amington, Tamworth, Staffordshire, B77 4RP

Rising Stars UK Ltd.
7 Hatchers Mews, Bermondsey Street, London SE1 3GS
www.risingstars-uk.com

Published 2012

Cover design: Burville-Riley Partnership
Brighton photographs: iStock
Illustrations: Chris King for Illustration Ltd (characters and cover artwork)/
Abigail Daker (map) http://illustratedmaps.info
Text design and typesetting: Geoff Rayner
Publisher: Rebecca Law
Editorial manager: Sasha Morton Creative Project Management

British Library Cataloguing in Publication Data.
A CIP record for this book is available from the British Library.

ISBN: 978-0-85769-605-2

Printed and bound by CPI Group (UK) Ltd, Croydon, CR0 4YY

MIX
Paper from
responsible sources
FSC
www.fsc.org   FSC® C020471

Contents

Name:
John Logan

Age:
24

Hometown:
Manchester

Occupation:
Author of
supernatural
thrillers

Special skills:
Not yet known

profiles

Name:
Rose Petal

Age:
22

Hometown:
Brighton

Occupation:
Yoga teacher,
nightclub and
shop owner,
vampire hunter

Special skills:
Private investigator
specialising in
supernatural
crime

Location map

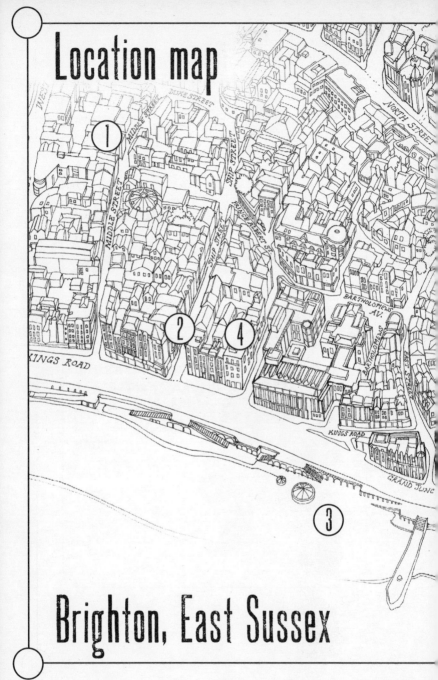

Brighton, East Sussex

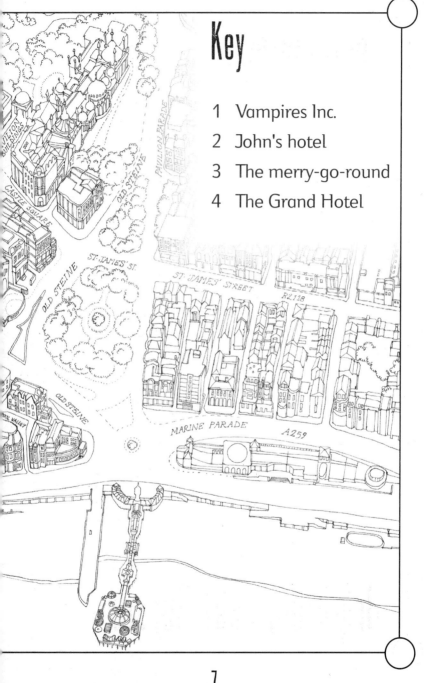

Key

1 Vampires Inc.
2 John's hotel
3 The merry-go-round
4 The Grand Hotel

Chapter 1

6 August, 1962

The sun was shining on Brighton's beaches. It was a lovely summer day. Tourists had flocked to Brighton Pier to visit its fortune-tellers, shows and fairground rides.

Mad Jack was the new ride at the funfair. A crowd of people watched the first car of happy riders climb up into the sky. The way back down was very steep. Everybody started to scream with excitement as the car dropped. Except the car did not turn at the sharp bend as it was supposed to. It tipped off the track and fell into the sea. So did the

next car and the one after it. Nearly
thirty people who were strapped into
their seats could not escape. The cars
sank to the bottom of the sea. No one
in the first three cars survived.

The seaside town was in shock that
day. It was the worst thing to ever
happen in Brighton.

6 August, this year

John Logan looked out of the window
of his hotel room. He watched families
laying down flowers at the end of the
pier. 'Those must be the families of
the people who died that day,' he said
to Rose Petal, his research assistant.
John was a writer who was finding out
more about the supernatural. Rose was

showing him the dark side of Brighton. A side full of vampires, werewolves and other strange beings that John was only just starting to understand.

'You know, after the accident, there was one girl who was never seen again,' Rose Petal said. 'Amy Porter went missing while her family was rescued from the ride. But every few years, people say they've seen her ghost. A little girl, frozen in time. Still the age she was in 1962. The police think someone took her away with them. Her family never saw her again.'

'Maybe she just lived on to be an old woman somewhere else,' said John.

'Or maybe something worse happened to her,' Rose Petal replied.

'You see, every few years, a child goes missing on the same date – the anniversary of the accident. I just can't believe that the new missing kids and Amy, or her ghost, aren't linked. They only go missing on the years that her ghost is seen. It freaks me out.'

Just then Rose's mobile phone rang. John watched her frown and ask a few questions. Finally, she ended the call with a sigh. 'A six-year-old girl went missing from the seafront merry-go-round last night. The parents think she might have been kidnapped.'

John checked the time. His sister and nephew were coming to stay with him for the weekend. John had to collect them from the train station.

'Call me later and let me know what's going on, okay?' he said.

****

Rose went to the police station and met the missing girl's parents. The police explained to them that Rose helped to investigate cases of missing persons. They didn't say that she also helped them to solve cases of vampire killings.

'Sarah had met a little girl called Alice at the merry-go-round,' said the child's mother. 'Alice was with her father. She was a sweet little thing with big blue eyes and blonde, curly hair.'

'Then what happened?' asked Rose.

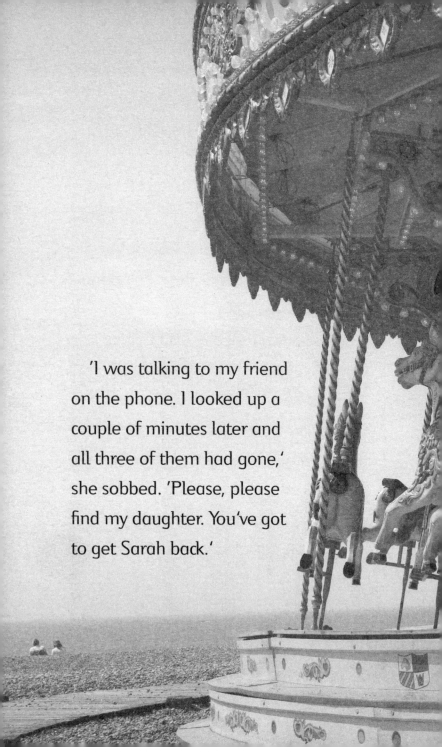

'I was talking to my friend on the phone. I looked up a couple of minutes later and all three of them had gone,' she sobbed. 'Please, please find my daughter. You've got to get Sarah back.'

Chapter 2

Saturday morning was cloudy again. John was looking after his nephew while his sister did some shopping. At a craft café under Brighton Pier, John ordered a juice for Tom and a coffee for himself. Soon, Tom had started drawing and another little girl joined him at his table. Her name was Alice.

John watched the children on and off while he drank his coffee and checked his emails. At first Alice and Tom did not talk. But then Alice put her arm round Tom's shoulder like an older sister.

'What are you drawing?' she asked.

'It's Victor the Vampire from TV,' said

Tom. 'He's my favourite vampire. He's funny.'

'Do you know a lot about vampires, Tom?' said Alice. Tom looked into her big, blue eyes. She seemed different to the girls from school.

Tom nodded. Alice sat next to him and started to whisper to him as she drew. John looked over again. Tom seemed happy. He sent Jenny a text:

To: Jenny
Tom's having a great time.
Stay out for lunch. We'll see
you back at the hotel later.
John x

Alice smiled. 'I know a lot about vampires,' she said. 'Can I draw on your picture, too?'

An hour later, John paid his bill and went over to collect Tom from the art table. He was on his own by now. A tall man in a dark suit and hat had come to take Alice home a few minutes before.

'Did you have a nice time?' he asked his nephew.

'Yes thanks, Uncle John. Look at my drawing. Alice helped me draw all the vampires she knows,' said Tom. As John looked at the picture a shiver went down his spine. He needed to take it to Rose right away.

Neither of them saw the woman in black watching them hurry away …

****

While Tom watched TV on Rose's sofa, John and Rose spoke to each other in whispers. Rose stared at the picture as John paced up and down. 'This is scary,' he said quietly. 'How could a six-year-old girl show a vampire killing in so much detail?'

'What I don't like is how the vampire killer is holding the hands of two children,' said Rose. 'One boy and one girl. And look at all the other kids behind the dead girl at the front here. There are seven children. The same number of kids that have gone missing since Amy Porter disappeared. I think this is the link we needed to find the missing girl. We just need to track down this man ...'

Rose also thought that the little boy holding the vampire's hand looked a lot like Tom. She didn't say that to John. Just then, Tom popped his head up over the back of the sofa. 'Are you talking about Alice's daddy?' said Tom.

Rose and John looked at each other in shock. 'Yes, Tom. Do you know where he and Alice live?'

'Alice said that they lived in a big, white house,' said Tom. 'There was a picture of it hanging on the wall in the café.'

'Do you think you would know the house again, Tom? Maybe if we found a picture on the computer?' asked Rose carefully. She and Tom clicked through some photos slowly. Finally, Tom shouted, 'That's it! Alice's house!' The photo was of the Grand Hotel — the biggest and most expensive hotel in Brighton. They had their lead.

Chapter 3

John and Rose sat on a bench eating ice cream with Tom, even though the day was gloomy and grey. 'I've got a plan,' said Rose Petal. 'The front desk will know which room Alice and her father are in. I want to search their room.'

'You can't just wander in and ask that, you're a total stranger. They'll never tell you anything,' said John.

'I know! That's why I'm finishing this ice cream before I start my shift,' grinned Rose. John was confused. He looked at her with raised eyebrows. 'Your shift?'

'My friend Kelly works here as a

maid. She's lent me her uniform and a key card so I can get into any room to clean it. I'll call you as soon as I'm done. Don't wait for me, it might take a while,' said Rose. She looked very pleased with her plan.

'Just keep safe. Don't do anything silly,' warned John.

Rose rolled her eyes at him. Then she stood up, waved goodbye to Tom and went to the staff entrance. John just hoped she would find the missing girl soon. A cloud passed over the sun and he shivered. He had a bad feeling about all of this.

As John and Tom started to walk back to their hotel, a woman tapped John on the arm.

'I must talk to you. I think I know what you are doing. I can help,' she said, in a nervous whisper. 'I'm Amy Porter's sister.'

John held on tightly to Tom's hand. 'Not in front of the boy,' he replied quietly.

'Very well, meet me at nine o'clock at the end of Brighton Pier. Bring the girl with red hair.'

With that, the woman walked away. John watched her go as Tom tugged his hand to leave.

****

Later that evening, Rose was back from the hotel. 'So I got chatting to one of the housekeepers about Alice.'

Rose was talking very quickly. She was really excited about everything she had found out at the hotel. 'Peter Brooks checked into the Grand Hotel last week. He comes back every few years in the summer with his daughter, Alice. Sometimes they bring another child, a family friend or relative, Mrs Cross reckons. They're always about the same age, six or seven. They stay for a few days, then they all leave until the next year. Mrs Cross comes from a line of witches, she has always thought there was something odd about them.'

'So the housekeeper is a witch and she thinks someone else is odd. That makes sense in this town,' said John. He took a deep breath. 'Look, Rose, I think we are dealing with a vampire and a vampire child.'

Rose nodded. 'Logan, you are spot on,' she said. 'Peter Brooks must spend a lot of time travelling around finding "friends" for his daughter to play with. She goes through a lot of them. Check this out!'

Rose showed John some pictures on her phone. She had found a diary in Alice and Peter's room and photographed some of the pages.

August 1972

Back in Brighton, ten years after I died. So bored. Daddy says he'll make me a new friend. Marie didn't last long after I took her out in the sun.

August 1987

There are lots of new friends to choose from this year for my birthday. I like the look of Nick. He's only five, but he reminds me of my little brother.

August 2002

I've been a vampire for forty years today but I still look six. I hate my life. I'm going to get my own present this year. I can change people now. Daddy doesn't like me doing it, but I don't care.

'We can't let them get away with this, Rose,' gasped John. 'Alice is a killer, just like her father!'

'Let's meet the woman tonight, see what she knows,' said Rose. 'We might be too late to find this year's missing girl, but we can stop it happening again.'

Chapter 4

Logan and Rose Petal went to the funfair at the end of Brighton Pier. A thick mist had shut the fair down for the night. For once, the pier was quiet and it felt spooky.

The woman was sitting in the last shelter on the pier. She was shivering in the fog. She introduced herself as Molly. John and Rose sat down with her.

'I couldn't stand seeing any more TV reports about missing children,' she explained. 'I remember what happened on the day Amy went missing like it was yesterday.'

'Go on, tell us,' said Rose Petal softly.

'Amy didn't want to go on Mad Jack. She was scared of heights. I went on it with my parents. I remember my mum telling Amy to wait by the ticket office for us. She told her we wouldn't be long. Then the car in front of us crashed into the sea. We were left hanging over the broken track. I thought I was going to die.'

'How long were you trapped on the ride for?' asked John.

'They were trying to rescue the people in the water. It must have been two hours before we got down. By then, Amy was gone. We never saw her again.' Molly wiped away a tear as Rose took her hand.

'You have seen your sister since then, haven't you?' said Rose.

Molly nodded. 'I've seen her many times,' she said. 'But it can't really be her. She's still the same age as the day she went missing. Every time I see her in Brighton, I call her name. She knows who I am but she runs away. She's so fast.'

Molly paused and looked up at John and Rose. 'That's not all. After I see her, children go missing. It's always the same pattern.'

Just then, John's phone rang. It was Jenny. 'Come quickly,' she sobbed. 'I've lost Tom. He's gone missing from the hotel.'

They left Molly and ran up the pier to

John's hotel. Jenny was pacing up and down in the lobby, crying.

'What happened?' asked Rose.

'I was checking my emails and Tom was over there.' Jenny pointed to a brightly lit fish tank in a corner of the hotel reception. 'A little girl was looking at the fish and Tom already knew her. When the girl left it seems like Tom went with her.'

'Did the girl have blue eyes and blonde, curly hair?' John asked.

Jenny nodded. John groaned. Rose Petal pulled Logan outside the hotel.

'Alice is staying in the penthouse at the Grand Hotel. We'll find them, Logan. I promise you,' she said. 'We'll get Tom back.'

Chapter 5

John and Rose ran along the seafront
to the Grand Hotel. They took the lift
straight to the top floor. Rose reached
into her rucksack and found a key card.
The door clicked open quietly and
they crept inside. They found Tom and
Sarah, the girl who went missing from
the seafront, watching the television.

'Tom, are you okay? Are you hurt?'
asked John. He checked Tom's and
Sarah's necks for bite marks. None
were there. 'How many times have
your mum and I told you not to talk to
strangers!'

'It was Alice and her dad, they're not

strangers,' Tom replied.

'Where's Alice?' asked Rose, looking around the room. She was holding a wooden stake in one hand.

'She's in the bathroom talking to her dad,' said Tom. 'He's not feeling well.'

They pushed open the door to the bathroom. Peter Brooks was lying on the floor. He was howling with pain and holding his stomach. Alice was sitting on the side of the bath, looking down at him. She was smiling.

'Shut the door,' said Logan. 'I don't want the kids to see what's going on in here. They're too young.'

'I'm just a little girl too,' said Alice slyly.

'Actually, you're a fifty-year-old

vampire,' said Rose. She moved towards Alice with the wooden stake raised.

'This man here made me what I am,' she said. 'But now he's dying. I gave him poisoned animal blood. He treats me like a child, but I'm in charge now. I've spent fifty years stuck in this body instead of being with my real family, using my real name. While they were trapped on the ride, he took me away and made me a vampire. I could never go home again. Not like this.'

'I can see why you're so angry,' said Rose. 'But killing him won't make you human again. It won't bring back your family.'

'I'm going to make my own family.

This time I'll look after them properly. Sarah and Tom will be my sister and brother forever,' she said.

'That's not going to happen,' shouted John. He pushed Alice down into the bath and held her down by the neck. 'Rose! Stake her!' he yelled. But Rose hesitated for just a moment. That was all the time Alice needed – even child vampires are too strong and too quick for humans.

With a scream, Alice leapt up in the air and scuttled like a spider across the ceiling. John fell backwards and tripped over Peter's curled-up body. Rose chased after the vampire child as she headed for the doors leading to the balcony.

Alice jumped from the balcony of the penthouse. They watched her fall down to the dark pavement below. As she fell, she rolled up into a little ball, then landed neatly on her feet. Without a backward glance, Alice ran off into the mist.

'Did you see that?' gasped Logan. 'Not bad for a six-year-old!'

'Even better for a fifty-year-old,' Rose replied. 'We need to clean up here. Peter Brooks is still dying in the bathroom. You take the kids. I'll deal with him and call the police to take Sarah back to her parents.'

'When you say "deal with him", do you mean ...?' asked John, quietly.

'Yes. He is beyond saving. And he

doesn't deserve it. It looks like Alice is getting what she wanted after all,' said Rose. She had already picked up the stake and was walking into the bathroom, closing the door firmly behind her.

****

That night, John walked alone by the sea. He felt so pleased to have Tom back again, he couldn't stop smiling.

Further up the beach, hidden by the mist, a woman was smiling too. She wandered along the pebbles, holding hands with her little sister. Alice looked up at Molly and grinned. She had found her real family at last. Now they could be together. Forever …

43

Glossary

anniversary – the date of an important event that you remember

confused – not knowing what to say or do

gasped – speaking with short breaths because a person is excited or frightened

pier – a long platform built into the sea, often with lots of shops and a funfair on it

tourists – visitors to a place who have come out for the day

Quiz

1   What was the name of the fairground ride that crashed in 1962?

2   How many people died in the fairground accident?

3   What was the name of the little girl who went missing on the day of the crash?

4   What is the name of the little girl who drew the pictures of the vampire killings?

5   Where do Alice and her father live?

6   Which of John Logan's relatives have come to stay with him in Brighton?

7   What does the vampire child Alice look like?

8   What does Alice do to her father to make him ill?

9   Why does Alice hate her father?

10 How does Alice escape?

Quiz answers

1 Mad Jack

2 About thirty

3 Amy Porter

4 Alice

5 The Grand Hotel

6 His sister, Jenny, and his nephew, Tom

7 She looks like a six-year-old with blonde, curly hair and blue eyes

8 She poisons him with animal blood

9 He turned her into a vampire when she was a little girl, so she has to stay that way forever

10 She jumps off the balcony of the hotel room and runs away

About the author

The author of these books teaches in a London school. At the weekend, his research takes him to the beaches and back streets of Brighton in search of werewolves and vampires.

He writes about what he has found.

 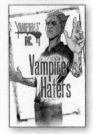